To my past and present
kindergarten students—you have
each brightened my room with your smiles,
enthusiasm and special talents!

JL

To my childhood friends 'le petit Paul,'
Camille, Hélène, Clément and Lian.

Qin

Published in 2013 by Simply Read Books www.simplyreadbooks.com
Text © 2013 Jennifer Lloyd · Illustrations © 2013 Qin Leng

Library and Archives Canada Cataloguing in Publication

Lloyd, Jennifer
        The best thing about kindergarten / written by
Jennifer Lloyd ; with illustrations by Qin Leng.

ISBN 978-1-897476-82-6

        I. Leng, Qin   II. Title.

PS8623.L69B47 2012   jC813'.6   C2011-900531-X

We gratefully acknowledge for their financial support of our publishing program the Canada Council for the Arts, the BC Arts Council, and the Government of Canada through the Canada Book Fund (CBF).

Manufactured in Malaysia

Book design by Natasha Kanji

10 9 8 7 6 5 4 3 2

The Best Thing About Kindergarten

BY JENNIFER LLOYD   ILLUSTRATED BY QIN LENG

SIMPLY READ BOOKS

It was the last day of kindergarten.

The students were getting ready for their graduation.

Mrs. Appleby looked at her class proudly. They had made fancy hats...

...and special decorations.

They
knew how
to sing their
graduation
song.

"Carpet places, everyone," Mrs. Appleby said. "We still have time for one last guessing game."

She waited for Tabitha to fix her hat...

...and for Jonathan to finish tying his shoe.

Then she began: "Who can guess what is the best thing about kindergarten?"

"It's calendar time!" cried Tabitha.

"You are so good at saying the days of the week," replied Mrs. Appleby, "but calendar time is not the best thing about kindergarten."

"It's the playhouse center!" exclaimed Corrine.

"The playhouse center is the perfect place for someone with
   your imagination, but keep on guessing!"

"The block corner!" proclaimed Benjamin.

"Your tunnels and towers are terrific," agreed Mrs. Appleby.

"Please put the blocks away, Benjamin. Something else is the best thing about kindergarten."

"How about arts and crafts time?" asked Clara.

"You can cut spectacular shapes. However, that's not the answer."

"It's definitely math time," piped up Adrien.
"One, two, three, four, five..."

"Great counting," said Mrs. Appleby. "Keep trying though. Something even better is the best thing about kindergarten."

"Could it be
the writing center?"
asked Patrick.

"You have learned many wonderful words. But beginning to write is not it, either."

For her guess, Emily held up a book.

"Emily, when I say *123 Storytime Zip* you are always ready to listen."

Suddenly the class sat very still.

"Oh, it is not storytime now," giggled Mrs. Appleby. "On with the guessing game." The students thought as hard as they could.

"Recess is the best!" declared Will, leading the others outside.

"You are a monkey bar superstar. But come back! We still haven't found the answer!"

Just then marching music drifted from the gym.

"Straighten your hats, everyone. Time to go."

The students
scurried into line, all
except Alex.

"We don't know the best thing about kindergarten," he protested.

Mrs. Appleby smiled. "I'll tell you soon."

"This is our graduation day! With much pride, we are on our way..." sang the students.

Their hats swished as they danced, keeping the beat to Mrs. Appleby's drum.

One by one, the children received their diplomas.

At the end of the ceremony, the audience clapped.
Mrs. Appleby clapped the loudest.

The children gathered near their teacher.

"What is the best thing about kindergarten?" they shouted together.

"It is each one of you, of course! You, my students, are
the best thing about kindergarten!" exclaimed Mrs. Appleby,
giving them all a great big graduation hug.